AMERICA'S WHITE TABLE

Margot Theis Raven - Illustrated by *Mike Benny*

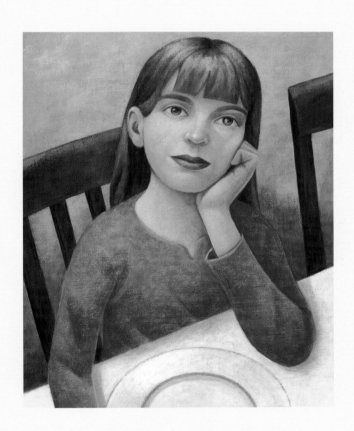

It was just a little white table...

but it brought tears of pride
to my Uncle John's eyes
the Veterans Day
he came for dinner
and stood by it
—set for one person—
even though nobody would be eating at it.

My country, 'tis of thee,

It was just a little white table...

but earlier that day Mama had told
Gretchen, Samantha, and me
the little table we were setting for
Veterans Day was just like the ones
that have stood across America
in the dining halls of the Army,
Navy, Marine Corps, and Air Force
since the Vietnam War ended.

The tables honor the men and women
who serve in America's Armed Forces
especially those missing in action—our MIAs,
and those held prisoner of war—our POWs.

Sweet land of liberty,

It was just a little white table...

but it felt as big as America when we helped Mama put
each item on it and she told us why it was so important.

"We use a small table, girls," she explained first,
"to show one soldier's lonely battle against many.
We cover it with a white cloth to honor a soldier's
pure heart when he answers his country's call to duty.

We place a lemon slice and grains of salt on a plate
to show a captive soldier's bitter fate and the tears of families
waiting for loved ones to return," she continued.

"We push an empty chair to the table
for the missing soldiers who are not here."

"We lay a black napkin for the sorrow of captivity,
and turn over a glass for the meal that won't be eaten," she said.

"We place a white candle for peace and finally, a red rose
in a vase tied with a red ribbon for the hope that
all our missing will return someday."

Mama finished speaking just as sunlight spilled on the table
and filled the overturned glass.

Of thee I sing;

It was just a little white table...

but it suddenly made me want to burst with
a feeling I couldn't explain when
Mama told us how much our setting
the white table would mean to Uncle John that night.
Then she told us something we didn't know:
Our Uncle John—
who gave us big bear hugs,
and spun us with airplane twirls,
and called me his Katie-girl...

...was a POW in Vietnam before we were born.

It was just a little white table...

but it gave us the courage to ask Mama
what happened to Uncle John in Vietnam.
She quietly told us his story.

*"When Uncle John served in Vietnam he was sent on a rescue mission,
and his helicopter was shot down behind enemy lines,"* she began.

Land where my fathers died,

"...and he and his three crew members were taken prisoner.

One crew member named Mike had serious wounds from the crash, but Uncle John and the other men tried to help Mike get better and persuaded a guard to bring Mike medicine.

Then one day when a guard looked away, Uncle John and the others had a chance to escape, but Mike was still too sick to go, so Uncle John stayed behind, because he wouldn't leave a fellow soldier alone so far from home."

Land of the pilgrims' pride,

"But how did Uncle John get free?" we asked Mama.

"Sometime later, Uncle John had a chance to escape again, and somehow he was able to take Mike with him, carrying him on his back and collecting just enough rainwater in big leaves to keep them alive until Uncle John found an American infantry unit to help them.

But even though Uncle John did everything he could to bring Mike home alive, Mike's wounds were just too serious and he died before the rescue helicopter landed.

I know that Mike was only 20 years old and he dreamed of playing football, but he loved America enough to give his life for his country when duty called.

And I know how much Uncle John loves America, too, but he learned when helping Mike that a soldier risks his life for a fellow soldier, because the best of your country lives in every man and woman who would lay down their life for you, too."

From every mountainside,

It was just a little white table...

but it needed words of gratitude, like Mama's Thanksgiving meal, so before Uncle John arrived for dinner, Gretchen and Samantha and I decided to put three gifts of our own on the table to honor our veterans.

Gretchen colored pictures of all the objects on the table, and Samantha wrote out the words of "My Country 'Tis of Thee" as a tribute in song.

But I didn't know what I—a ten-year-old-girl—could *ever* put on the table that was as important as each veteran's gift of freedom to me.

It was just a little white table...

but I looked at it all dinner long,
and in the quiet inside me
I could almost hear the silent soldiers
of the empty chair saying:

Remember us, please...
we are real people like your Uncle John and Mike
who left families and friends, homes and dreams of our own
to protect your birthright of liberty from disappearing
as easily as sunlight from a glass.

Let freedom ring!

It was just a little white table...

But it took my words away when I hugged
Uncle John good night and wanted to thank him
for serving our country so bravely.
So I just hugged him even harder and told him
I loved him.

Uncle John hugged me back even harder
than I had hugged him.

And that's when I knew what I could put on the table:
My promise to put the words from my heart into a little book
about America's White Table.
And in the book I'd use Gretchen's pictures and Samantha's song
and Mama's story about Uncle John and his friend Mike—
because I hoped that everyone who read it
would set a white table on Veterans Day, too—
so the brave Americans the little table honors
won't ever feel forgotten by the country they loved so much.

Then in the salt
on the little white table...

I traced in the grains of their families' tears—
what each man and woman who
serves America is to me, a...

Hero

And that's when I saw
the tears of pride
fill my Uncle John's eyes.

THE HISTORY OF THE WHITE TABLE

The POW story of Uncle John and his cell mate Mike was purposely not based on any one particular story, but rather was compiled from different service members' acts of heroism during the Vietnam War. This choice was made to allow *America's White Table* to represent every branch of the military, and be a universal sign of brotherhood for all MIAs and POWs.

As a symbol of missing and captive service members, the MIA/POW table originated during the time of the Vietnam War. All known American prisoners of war (POWs) were released in 1973, following the Paris Peace Agreement between North Vietnam, South Vietnam, and the United States. While the agreement ended the long war, open wounds were left in America's national consciousness. An unpopular war in America, the Vietnam War brought hard times to our nation and even more so to its veterans. The soldiers and military personnel sent to serve there in active combat returned to an unfriendly homeland that largely didn't honor their service and sacrifice of self on foreign soil.

However, out of those troubling times came new outward symbols of caring for our MIA and POW service members. Initiated by loving family members and concerned organizations, these outward symbols included: POW bracelets, yellow ribbons, a POW flag, and the MIA/POW Remembrance or Missing Man Table.

A group called the Red River Valley Fighter Pilots Association or the River Rats set the first MIA/POW Remembrance Table. During the Vietnam War this daring group of airmen came from different branches of America's armed forces. They took their name from missions flown into North Vietnam and the combat zone surrounding Hanoi along the Red River. The missions were dangerous, and pilots took strength from their brotherhood of courage and shared knowledge.

In the spirit of that brotherhood, the River Rats pledged themselves to taking care of their own and having reunions once the war ended and the POWs came home, but initially held practice "reunions" while still in Southeast Asia and America. It was at the first practice "reunion," that the MIA/POW table was set in remembrance of fallen and missing comrades. (The Red River Valley Fighter Pilots Association is still in active existence today, providing scholarship money to children of airmen killed during training or missing and killed in action in America's conflicts.)

Following the Vietnam War, the tradition of the Remembrance Table then made its way into all military dining-in/dining out ceremonies (dinners where members of a command, unit, or other organization gather, including with spouses and guests).

At the ceremonies, a series of toasts are made before being seated to eat, with the last toast, "to remember until they come home," reserved for (and always made with water) their comrades of the MIA/POW table.

Sometimes the items on the table vary from ceremony to ceremony; for example, uniform hats from all the service branches can be placed around the table. Sometimes the exact symbolic meaning of the items differ slightly, too, but generally the words that Mama told Katie, Samantha, and Gretchen are standard, giving touching tribute to our finest and bravest countrymen—those who wait, and hope and believe in the dream of freedom with every breath they take on foreign soil, and whose spirits live beyond the chains of their prisons.

In this book we salute these bravest of our brave with the POW flag motto:

YOU ARE NOT FORGOTTEN
SO LONG AS THERE IS ONE LEFT IN WHOM YOUR MEMORY REMAINS.

....

To honor those who have served in our country's armed forces, America observes two national holidays:

Memorial Day: *Observed on the last Monday in May in honor of veterans no longer living.*
Veterans Day: *Always observed on November 11 in honor of all veterans, but particularly those still living.*

Although not an official national holiday, by presidential proclamation our country has observed National MIA/POW Recognition Day since 1979. That day is held on the third Friday in September to honor the sacrifice of America's POWs and MIAs and their families, and to address the fate of troops still unaccounted for in conflict since the First World War.

To the Red River Valley Fighter Pilots Association who set the first white table;
To Charleston Air Force Base who first showed it to me;
And to all men and women in uniform who dedicate their lives
to freedom's cause — especially, TJH, my hero.

MARGOT

For Mary Ann, Adele, and Hank, with all my love and adoration.

MIKE

"My Country 'Tis of Thee"
Words: Samuel F. Smith, 1832

Sleeping Bear Press

Sleeping Bear Press
310 North Main Street, Suite 300
Chelsea, MI 48118
www.sleepingbearpress.com

THOMSON
GALE

© 2005 Thomson Gale, a part of the Thomson Corporation.

Thomson, Star Logo and Sleeping Bear Press are trademarks
and Gale is a registered trademark used herein under license.

Printed and bound in Canada.

10 9 8 7 6 5 4 3 2 1

Library of Congress Cataloging-in-Publication Data

Raven, Margot Theis.
America's white table / written by Margot Theis Raven ;
illustrated by Mike Benny.
p. cm.
Summary: Three children set a special white table in memory of
service members fallen or missing in action, and especially in honor
of their Uncle John, a POW in Vietnam.
ISBN 1-58536-216-6
[1. Rites and ceremonies—Fiction. 2. Veterans—Fiction. 3. Heroes—Fiction.
4. Tables—Fiction. 5. Uncles—Fiction.] I. Benny, Mike.
1964- , ill. II. Title.
PZ7.R1955Am 2005
[Fic]—dc22   2004027835